TALES of the UGLY OGRES

retold by
Corinne Denan

illustrated by
Kinuko Craft

Troll Associates

Tales of the Ugly Ogres: Hop O' My Thumb, Perrault.

Copyright © 1980 by Troll Associates, Mahwah, N.J.

Library of Congress # 79-66333
ISBN 0-89375-332-7/0-89375-331-9 (pb)

CONTENTS

The Count and the Fox

Once upon a time there was a young man who was very lazy. He never did anything his parents asked him to do.

Before the young man's father died, he said, "Son, you will soon be left alone in the world with nothing but this small cottage and the pear tree that grows behind it. You must go to work, or else you will starve."

But the lazy young man did not go to work. He was content just to sit outside his small cottage and eat the fruit of the pear tree. Unlike other such trees, this one could bear fruit the year round. And moreover, the fruit was the finest in the land.

One day a sly fox passed the cottage. He saw the young man dozing under the pear tree.

"I have never seen such fine pears," said the fox. "If you will be so kind as to give me one basket full, it will bring you luck."

The young man was lazy, but he was not foolish. "If I give you a basket of pears," he said, "then what am I to eat?"

"Trust me," answered the fox, "and luck will be yours."

The young man was too lazy to argue. So he gave the fox a basket of the ripest pears. "Thank you, kind sir," said the fox. And off he went.

The fox trotted straightaway to the palace of the King. Bowing graciously, the fox said, "My master sends you a few of his finest pears, your majesty. He begs you to accept them." And with that, the fox laid the delicious fruit before the King.

"And just who is your master?" inquired the King.

"He is the Count," said the fox.

"What may I send the Count in return for this delicious fruit?" the King asked.

"Merely your thanks, kind Ruler," said the fox. And he went away.

Some time later, the fox returned to the lazy young man. "I want another basket of pears," he said.

Once more the young man said to him, "And then what shall I have to eat?"

"Fear not, and trust me," said the fox. This time the fox himself picked a basket of fruit, bigger than the last. And with the basket in his mouth, he trotted off to the palace. Once again, he asked to see the King.

"Your majesty, my master the Count once

more sends his respects by offering this basket of pears."

"I cannot understand this," said the King. "Snow is now deep upon the ground. How can he grow these delicious pears?"

"Oh, my master the Count is rich enough to grow anything," said the fox in a sly manner.

"How can I repay him?" asked the King.

"Well," said the fox, "this time he would ask for your daughter's hand in marriage."

"Well, that may be a problem," said the King thoughtfully. "Perhaps you could ask him to come to the palace so we might talk."

The fox bowed out of the throne room and trotted back to the cottage. There he found the lazy young man asleep.

"Wake up," said the fox. "I've told the King that you are a Count, and you are going to marry his daughter."

"What have you done, fox?" the young man cried. "The minute the King sees me, he will have my head cut off!"

"Don't worry about that," said the fox. "Just do what I say and luck will be with you."

Then the fox trotted into town and banged on the door of the tailor.

"My master the Count needs the finest of your

garments," said the fox, putting on a very grand air. "He is off for an audience with the King. If the coat fits him, I will pay for it tomorrow."

Now the tailor had never once made anything for a Count before, and so he was much impressed. "He will have a choice of my finest," said the tailor.

The fox chose a garment of silver and white. The tailor wrapped it up carefully, and the fox carried it off. His next stop was the horse trader's shop. There he talked the merchant into sending his finest horse to the cottage.

When the young man saw the silver and white coat and the fine horse, he was very surprised. But, at the fox's urging, he put on the coat and mounted the horse.

"What am I to say to his majesty?" asked the young man. "I have never spoken to a King before."

"Just be quiet," said the fox. "Leave the talking to me." And off they went to the palace.

The King himself came out to greet the young man. He led him into the great hall, where a banquet had been prepared. There at the table sat a beautiful Princess. The young man fell in love with her at once, and she fell in love with him.

The young man uttered hardly a word all during dinner. During dessert, the King said to the fox, "Your master certainly does not talk much."

"His mind is on matters of property," said the fox quickly. "He has no time for chatter."

The King was quite impressed, and he said nothing more himself.

The very next morning, the fox came around to the cottage again. "Give me another basket of pears," he said.

"If the King ever finds out the truth about me, it will cost me my life," said the young man.

"Just leave things to me. I will bring you luck," the fox assured him.

And off went the fox to the King. "The Count sends you more of his finest fruit, and asks an answer to his proposal."

"Tell the Count that my daughter will be most happy to marry him, and I give my consent," said the King.

So the fox told the young man what the King had said. "But where will we live?" cried the young man. "I can't expect a Princess to live in this tiny cottage."

"Just leave everything to me," said the fox.

It took about a week for all the preparations to be made for the wedding. And then the young man and the Princess were married. After a week of feasting, the fox said to the King, "My master wishes to return to his castle with his bride."

"Very well," said the King. "I will go with you to see where my daughter is going to live."

And so the King and his soldiers and the young man and the Princess all set out. The fox ran on ahead.

When the fox saw a rich herd of sheep along the way, he asked the shepherd, "To whom do these sheep belong?"

The shepherd replied, "To the evil Ogre."

"Do you see those soldiers riding behind me?" said the fox. "They will kill the sheep if they know the Ogre owns them. You must say that they belong to the Count."

Soon the King rode up and asked the shepherd whose fine sheep he guarded. "The Count's sheep," said the shepherd. And the King was much impressed.

Next the fox saw a rich herd of pigs. "To whom do these pigs belong?" he asked of the swineherd.

"They belong to the evil Ogre," the swineherd said.

The fox said, "The soldiers behind me will kill

them unless you say that the pigs belong to the Count."

When the King asked who owned the pigs, the swineherd said, "They belong to the Count."

"My son-in-law must truly be rich," thought the King.

Soon the fox came to the Ogre's castle. He threw himself on the castle steps as the Ogre ran out. "What a sad fate has befallen you!" wailed the fox.

"What are you talking about?" said the Ogre, who was truly evil. He was also rather cowardly.

"The King has sent a troop of soldiers to kill you," said the fox. "The best place for you to hide is in your huge oven."

So the evil Ogre hid in the huge oven. Then the fox put down the latch and roasted him without a moment's thought.

Soon the King and his party rode up to the castle. "To whom does this splendid castle belong?" asked the King.

"Why, to the Count, of course," said the fox.

The King was very impressed. The next morning he rode off to his own castle, well pleased with his daughter's marriage.

The fox said to the young man, "Now that you are rich and happy, you no longer need me. But I ask one promise of you in return for what I have done. When I die, bury me in a fine coffin with great honors."

So the Count and the Princess stayed in the beautiful castle. They lived happily for many long years. And when the fox died, the Count gave him a fine silver coffin and buried him with great honors.

Hop O' My Thumb

Once there was a woodcutter and his wife, and they had seven sons. They were very poor. Their children were a great worry to them, for even the eldest was too young to earn a living.

But their greatest worry was their youngest son. He was very delicate and small. He was so small that when he was born he measured no bigger than a person's thumb. And so they called him Hop O' My Thumb.

Even though Hop O' My Thumb was very small, he was the wisest of the seven children. For he listened a good deal, and he learned much.

It so happened that there was a great famine in the land. The crops died in the fields. There was nothing at all for the woodcutter and his family to eat.

One night as he sat before a small fire, the woodcutter said, "We can no longer feed our children. But I cannot bear to watch them die of hunger. Tomorrow we will take them all to the woods to gather twigs. And then we shall lose them."

"Oh, no!" cried his wife. "I cannot bear to lose my children!" But finally, she consented to the plan.

Now it happened that when Hop O' My Thumb had heard his parents talking before the fire, he had crept under his father's chair. He was so small that he could not be seen. And he had heard every word they said. After his parents finished talking, he crept back to bed. And there he lay awake all night thinking of a plan.

Very early the next morning, Hop O' My Thumb left the house and ran down to the river's edge. There he picked up white pebbles and filled his pockets with them.

Later that morning, the woodcutter and his wife took their seven children into the forest. The seven sons began to gather twigs to tie into bundles. Soon, the parents saw that the children were busy, so they ran off through the forest.

When the children realized that they were alone, they began to cry. But Hop O' My Thumb said, "Cheer up, my brothers, for I can lead you home. When we left our house this morning, I dropped white pebbles all along the path. Now we will follow them."

And so Hop O' My Thumb led his brothers

back to their home. They could hear their parents talking inside, and they sat down near the door to listen.

It seems that when the woodcutter and his wife had returned from the woods, they had found a bag of money on the doorstep. It was payment for some work they had done long ago. The wife had gone straight to the butcher's and had brought home enough food for ten people.

Now the wife said to the woodcutter, "Alas— where are our poor children? We have more than enough food for them all. I told you it was wrong to leave them in the forest. Perhaps the wolves have eaten them already."

The woodcutter could not comfort his wife. She began to cry very loudly. "Alas, alas, where are our children?" she sobbed.

She cried so loud that the children, who were still sitting near the door, jumped up and cried, "Here we are! Here we are!"

Their mother ran to the door and embraced them all. "Oh, how happy I am to see you again, dear children," she said. "You must be tired and hungry. Come in, and I shall feed you well."

Everyone rejoiced because the family was together once more. The children ate a fine meal. And all slept well that night.

But, unhappily, the joy could not last. For the money was soon gone. And once again there was very little food for the table.

"There is nothing else to do," said the woodcutter sadly. "We must take the children deeper into the forest and lose them once more."

Again Hop O' My Thumb had crept under his father's chair and heard the plan. And again he rose early in the morning to collect pebbles. But this time he found the door locked. And since he was so small, he could not open it.

At first little Hop O' My Thumb did not know what to do. But he was wise, and soon came up with a plan. When the woodcutter gave each child a piece of bread for breakfast, Hop O' My Thumb put his in his pocket. He would drop crumbs along the way. The children could follow the crumbs home, just as they had followed the pebbles.

This time the woodcutter and his wife led the children deeper into the forest. Then they left them, and stole off as before.

Hop O' My Thumb was not worried. He would lead his brothers back home by following the bread crumbs. But to his great sorrow, he found that the birds had eaten every crumb. There was no path to follow.

The brothers began to cry. Hop O' My Thumb climbed to the top of a tall tree and saw a light in the middle of the forest.

"Let us walk toward the light," he said.

At last the children came to a house in the forest. They knocked on the door, and a woman answered.

"We are lost in the forest," Hop O' My Thumb told her. "We have come to beg for a night's rest."

"Oh, my poor children," said the good woman, "you have come to the house of a cruel Ogre. He often eats youngsters like you."

Hop O' My Thumb and his brothers shook from head to toe when they heard that. But Hop O' My Thumb said to the woman, "Where can we go? If we stay in the forest tonight, surely the wolves will eat us."

Now the good woman, who was the wife of the Ogre, felt very sorry for them. She thought that perhaps she could hide them through the night, and so she let them enter.

The seven brothers began to warm themselves by a huge fire. An entire sheep was roasting over the fire for the Ogre's supper.

Just then, they heard three sharp blows at the

door. The Ogre had come home. Quickly his wife hid the children under the bed.

The Ogre walked in and sat down at the table. Then he began to sniff the air about him. "I smell raw meat," he said in a booming voice.

"What you smell," said his wife, "must be this meat I am roasting for your supper."

"I tell you I smell *raw* meat!" roared the Ogre. He jumped up and went straight for the bed. He dragged out the frightened children, one by one. They fell upon their knees and begged for mercy.

But the Ogre would not listen to their pleas. Instead, he began to sharpen his great knife.

"Why are you in such a hurry?" asked his wife. "You have plenty of roast meat for tonight. Why not save the children for tomorrow?"

"A good idea," agreed the Ogre. "Fatten them up for me."

So the wife gave the brothers a hearty meal. But they were so terrified that they barely touched their food. Then she put them to bed with sleeping caps upon their heads.

Now it happened that the Ogre had seven young daughters. They were beginning to look a good deal like their father. They were not yet as wicked as he, but they had already bitten several small children.

Hop O' My Thumb saw that the seven daughters were asleep. Fearing that the Ogre might kill him and his brothers during the night, he took the seven sleeping caps, and put them on the Ogre's daughters.

The Ogre did arise during the night, intending to kill the boys. In the dark, he felt for the seven sleeping caps. And, quick as a wink, that was the end of all seven daughters.

Well pleased with himself, the Ogre went back to sleep. Hop O' My Thumb then woke his brothers. They stole out of the house and quickly ran into the forest.

In the morning, the Ogre told his wife to wake their daughters so he might see them before he left for his day's work. When his wife saw what had happened, she fainted dead away. The Ogre came running. He could not believe his eyes.

"What have I done?" he roared. "Those wretches shall pay for this with their lives!"

Then he threw a bucket of water on his wife to revive her. "Get me my seven-league boots," he roared.

The wife brought them, and the Ogre set out. He could quickly travel great distances in his seven-league boots. After he had searched the

entire countryside, he came to the road that led to the woodcutter's house. The children had already found it, and now they were almost home.

When the boys heard the Ogre striding toward them, they hid behind some rocks. The Ogre did not see them, so he lay down to rest.

As soon as the Ogre was asleep, Hop O' My Thumb told his brothers to continue toward home. Then he crept softly up to the Ogre and pulled off the seven-league boots. Because the boots were magic, they fit anyone who wore them.

Hop O' My Thumb put the boots on, and ran back to the Ogre's house. "A band of robbers has seized your husband," he said to the Ogre's wife. "Unless you give me all your gold and silver, they will kill him." Of course, the Ogre's wife gave him the gold and silver.

Then Hop O' My Thumb caught up with his brothers, and continued home. How happy their parents were to see them!

"We should never have sent you away," they said. "But with all this gold and silver, we shall never have to worry about you again. And you, Hop O' My Thumb, have proven yourself the wisest of all our children."

And indeed, the woodcutter and his wife and seven children lived happily ever after. And, the Ogre was so upset over the loss of his seven daughters that he never ate another child again, as long as he lived.

The Ogre, the Stone and the Clever Cat

Once there was a poor old man who lived with his wife and son at the edge of the plain. One day he fell ill and knew that his time was near. He said to his son, "I have nothing to leave you but my falcon bird, my greyhound dog, and my clever cat. But if you use them well, you will never lack for anything." And with that, the old man turned his face to the wall and died.

Some time later, the son was out hunting with the falcon, the greyhound, and the cat. Suddenly he felt a heavy hand upon his shoulder. To his surprise, an Ogre stood behind him.

"Good day, young man," said the Ogre pleasantly. "You have been a good son to your parents, and you deserve a reward. Come with me to the lake. Fear nothing."

Thinking that this must be a kindly Ogre, the young man followed him to the lake.

"Step into the water," the Ogre told him. "Sink to the bottom. But do not be afraid. At the bottom of the lake there is much silver. Bring up as much as you can carry. We will divide it between us."

The young man did as he was told. Soon he was sinking into the cold lake. When his feet touched the bottom, he opened his eyes. There in front of him were heaps of silver. And right in the middle was a strange white stone. It had curious markings on it. The young man picked up the stone to look at it. To his amazement, it began to speak to him.

"As long as you hold me, all your wishes will come true," said the stone. "Now hide me in your clothes and go back to the Ogre."

The Ogre was waiting at the edge of the lake. "Where is the silver?" he asked.

"Alas," said the young man, "I was so bewitched by the sight of the silver that I could not move. Then I heard steps behind me, and I became frightened. So I came up quickly."

The Ogre was very angry. "You are no better than the others I have asked to share the silver!" he shouted. And he stomped off in a great rage.

As soon as the Ogre was gone, the young man took out the stone and made a wish. "I want a fine camel to ride," he said, "and splendid clothes to wear."

"Shut your eyes," said the stone.

The young man shut his eyes. When he opened them, a great camel was standing before

34

him. And he found himself dressed in the beautiful robes of a Prince. The young man climbed upon the camel's back. The falcon sat on his wrist, and the greyhound and the cat followed along behind.

When the young man rode up to his home, his mother did not recognize him. Thinking he must be a Prince, she bowed her head.

Her son laughed. "Do you not know me, Mother?" he asked.

When his mother saw who stood before her, she nearly fell into a faint. "Surely you have stolen this fine camel and these beautiful clothes," she said.

"Fear not, Mother," replied the young man. "I have come by them honestly. I will explain everything to you later. First, I would like you to go to the palace and tell the King that I wish to marry his daughter."

The young man's mother thought he had gone mad. But her son said to her, "Do not fear. Whatever the King asks, tell him it will be done."

So the mother went to the palace and asked to see the King. "My son wants to marry the Princess," she said.

The King looked at the old woman for a moment, thinking she was mad. But because she

was so old, he decided to joke with her. "Very well, good woman," said the King. "Tell your son that he may marry the Princess if he builds a palace of ice that can be warmed with fires and where the rarest of singing birds can live."

"As you wish, your majesty," said the mother.

Her son was waiting outside the palace gates. "What must I do, Mother?" he asked.

"You must get this Princess out of your head," she said. "You can never do what the King asks."

"What is it?" asked the son.

"The King wants you to build a palace of ice that can be warmed with fires and where the rarest of singing birds can live."

"Ho!" laughed the young man. "Is that all? I thought it would be much harder. I must see about this at once."

So the young man left his mother and walked away. As soon as he was alone, he took out the stone. "I want a palace of ice that can be warmed with fires and where the rarest of singing birds can live," he said.

"Shut your eyes," said the stone.

When the young man opened his eyes, he stood before a magnificent ice palace. The fires inside glowed warmly. And the sound of rare singing birds could be heard.

"Fit indeed for a Princess," said the young man.

The King was very impressed when he saw the ice castle outside his window the next morning. "The young man must be a great wizard," he thought.

The Princess and the young man were married the very next day, and they moved into the ice palace.

About a month after the wedding, the young man decided to go hunting. He rode off with the falcon on his wrist and the greyhound and the cat following along behind.

No sooner had the young man left than the Ogre knocked at the palace door. He had been waiting his chance for days.

"I have been to a far country," he told the Princess. "And I have returned with precious jewels. I know that a Princess enjoys such things."

The Ogre laid before her the purest of pearls and the most sparkling of diamonds. "I really do not wish to sell them," he said. "But I have a necklace of stones given to me by my father. One of the stones is missing. It has strange markings on it. I have heard it is in your husband's posses-

sion. If you can get the stone for me, you may have any of these jewels you wish. But you must pretend that you want the stone for yourself. Your husband would never part with it for a stranger." And with that, the Ogre left.

The Princess loved her husband. But she was still young and a bit foolish. And not many Princesses can resist the thought of owning rare and beautiful jewels. So that evening at dinner, she said to her husband, "Tomorrow is my birthday"—which indeed it was. "You have given me much already, but there is one thing I wish for."

The young man was very much in love with his beautiful wife. And so he said, "Name it, and it shall be yours."

"I wish for that bright stone you carry with you," she said. "The one with the strange marks on it. I have never seen such a stone before."

The young man thought for a while. Then he said, "I promised, and so I shall keep my promise. But swear that you will never part from the stone. Swear that you will keep it safely with you always. More I cannot tell you. But I beg you to heed my words."

The Princess began to feel uneasy. But she pretended to be delighted with the stone. "I re-

ally don't have to give it to the Ogre," she said to herself.

The next day the young man went off to the hunt as before. And the Ogre came to the palace door. The Princess truly meant to keep the stone. But as soon as she saw the precious jewels once again, she could not take her eyes off them.

"Do you have the stone?" the Ogre asked.

"Here it is," she said. At the same time she thought to herself, "What is so important about the stone, anyway?" She gave the stone to the Ogre. Then she selected a rare string of pearls. And the Ogre left the palace.

But as soon as the Ogre had gone, a curious thing began to happen. The room began to feel chilly. The fires began to die out. The walls became wet and runny. The palace of ice had begun to melt!

When the young man returned, he stood horrified before the small pile of ice that had been the palace. And he knew at once that his wife had betrayed him. In anger, he took her back to her father's palace. "You have betrayed me," he said. "Now I must seek my fortune alone."

With the falcon and the greyhound and the cat, the young man went looking for the Ogre. But no one had seen him. Then the young man sent the falcon into the sky. The falcon flew so high that it was gone for a day and a night. When it returned, it said, "The Ogre is asleep in a great palace in a far country at the edge of the sea."

The young man said to the falcon, "Fly to the Ogre's palace and search for the stone while he is asleep."

"I must take the cat with me," said the falcon.

High into the air flew the falcon with the cat sitting firmly on its back. "Shut your eyes," the falcon warned. For the cat had never been off the ground except to climb a tree.

They flew all night until the Ogre's palace lay beneath them. "Aha!" said the cat, "I see that the Ogre's palace is overrun with rats."

Once on the ground, the cat immediately pounced on a rat. "Spare me, spare me," the rat squeaked.

"I will spare you all," said the clever cat, "if you find a strange white stone that the Ogre carries. Take it from him while he sleeps and bring it to me."

A few hours later, the rat returned with the stone. The cat spared all the rats. Then the cat and the falcon began their homeward journey. But since they were both tired, they stopped to rest near a river bank.

"Let me carry the stone for a while," said the falcon. "Otherwise our master will think I have done nothing."

"No, I will keep it," said the cat. They started to quarrel, and the cat dropped the stone. It fell into the river and right into the mouth of a large fish that was swimming by.

"Now what will we do?" gasped the falcon.

At once, the clever cat began to throw dirt into the river.

"What are you doing?" the falcon asked.

"I'm going to fill up the river so all the fish will die. Then I can find the stone," said the cat in a very loud voice.

Just as the clever cat had hoped, some of the fish in the river heard what he said. "We'll find the stone," they called out in alarm. They certainly did not want the cat to fill up the river.

All the fish began to swim this way and that. Finally, they found a dark, quiet corner of the river. And they saw an old tuna, who was resting there. When they told him what they were looking for, he said, "I do believe I swallowed something strange a while back." He coughed, and out popped the magic stone.

And so the clever cat and the falcon flew back

to the young man. How happy he was to see them and the stone!

The clever cat and the falcon, and the greyhound, too, were well cared for all their lives. The young man wished for a new palace. Then he forgave the Princess, for he truly loved her. The Princess never made such a mistake again. And they lived happily for many, many years.